by Paul Needs

Illustrated by Colin Wyatt

One day while I was digging in my garden, I discovered a village of little flowerpots. In this village lived the Poddington Peas.

The Peas soon became my friends, and began to tell me stories of their adventures. In return I promised to keep the secret of where they lived.

This is one of the many stories they told me.

Today was a very exciting day in the village of Poddington. It was the Annual Vegetable Show.

Slop-Pea was putting the finishing touches to a large sign advertising the event.

He stepped back to admire his handiwork.

All of a sudden, Zip-Pea, the fastest Pea in Poddington, came zooming past. He whooshed by so fast that poor Slop-Pea was spun around. The paint pot flew into the air and landed neatly on his head, just like a little hat.

'Oh, sorry Slop-Pea,' said Zip-Pea. 'Can you tell me, is this where the Show is being held?'

Slop-Pea looked up as a large blob of paint dripped onto his nose. 'Yes, Zip-Pea, it's over there,' he said.

Zip-Pea zoomed up to the large wooden stand where Garden Pea was busy polishing the Poddington Trophy Cup. This was the prize awarded each year to the winner of the Vegetable Show.

'I think my runner beans have a good chance of winning First Prize,' he said to Garden Pea.

'Well I wish you luck,' chuckled Garden Pea.

'Thank you very much,' said Zip-Pea, as he placed his runner beans on the stand and raced off.

Behind a bush the two naughty Peas, Creep-Pea and Black-eyed Pea, were watching carefully.

'I really want to win that cup,' said Creep-Pea.

'But Boss, we haven't grown anything and the Show is this afternoon,' said Black-eyed Pea. 'Even Zip-Pea couldn't grow anything that quickly.'

But Creep-Pea had a plan. He and Black-eyed Pea made their way back through the Creepy Carrot Patch to Creepy Castle which overlooked Poddington.

Garden Pea greeted the other Peas as they arrived at his stand with their entries for the Show.

Jump-Pea jumped up onto the stage with his spring greens. They were almost as springy as him. He was followed by tiny Wee McPea, who had brought along his dwarf French beans. Chip-Pea turned up with a large potato, which later she planned to fry into lovely fat chips. Sweet-Pea and Hap-Pea arrived together carrying their sweetcorn.

Suddenly the stand was covered by a large shadow as Dump-Pea, the fattest Pea in Poddington, arrived with his entry. It was a huge marrow that was even bigger than he was.

The whole village had turned out for the Show. Even Bump-Pea had arrived with a rather squashed plum.

The only one missing was Sleep-Pea and his bedding plants. As usual he had overslept.

Just then Creep-Pea and Black-eyed Pea came struggling through the Creepy Carrot Patch. They were pushing and pulling a wheelbarrow that contained the biggest tomato you have ever seen.

They struggled and wobbled past P.C. Pod who thought it made a nice change to see the two naughty Peas getting involved in village events.

Just as Garden Pea announced that the Show was open, Creep-Pea and Black-eyed Pea arrived with their huge wobbly tomato. They placed it in the middle of the stand and stood back to admire their work.

All the Peas were very impressed, all except P.C. Pod, who thought there was something very suspicious about Creep-Pea and Black-eyed Peas' wobbly tomato!

The Peas looked on in suspense as Garden Pea began judging the vegetables.

He marked his list for colour, looks and size.

Finally, after much thought, Garden Pea decided upon the winner.

'I am pleased to announce that the winners of the Poddington Vegetable Show, are Creep-Pea and Black-eyed Pea.'

The two Peas jumped onto the stage to collect their prize. They were very pleased that the Poddington Trophy Cup was theirs at last.

But as Garden Pea pinned the winner's rossette to the tomato there was a loud bang.

The tomato wasn't a tomato at all. It was a big red balloon which the two naughty Peas had filled with red paint.

'Oh no, that's blown it,' said Creep-Pea, as he and Black-eyed Pea stood dripping paint all over the stage. 'Time for a quick getaway.'

P.C. Pod chased Creep-Pea and Black-eyed Pea all the way back to Creepy Castle.

Garden Pea looked at his notes again to see who the real winner of the cup was.

'The new winner is Dump-Pea and his magnificent marrow,' he announced.

A delighted Dump-Pea struggled onto the stage to collect his prize.

All the Peas cheered as Dump-Pea posed proudly with the Poddington Trophy Cup.

Snap-Pea, the village photographer, took his picture for the front page of the *The Daily Pod*.